Priscilla's Paw de Deux

For the dancers at Jump To It
S J

For the dancers at The Dance Inn
L H

Text copyright © 2002 by Sharon Jennings
Illustrations copyright © 2002 by Linda Hendry

Design by Wycliffe Smith Design

Published in Canada by Fitzhenry & Whiteside, 195 Allstate Parkway, Markham, Ontario L3R 4T8

Published in the United States by Fitzhenry & Whiteside, 121 Harvard Avenue, Suite 2, Allston, Massachusetts 02134

www.fitzhenry.ca   godwit@fitzhenry.ca.

10 9 8 7 6 5 4 3 2 1

National Library of Canada Cataloguing in Publication

Jennings, Sharon
Priscilla's paw de deux / by Sharon Jennings ; illustrated by Linda Hendry.

ISBN 1-55041-718-5 (bound).--ISBN 1-55041-720-7 (pbk.)

I. Hendry, Linda II. Title.

PS8569.E563 P76 2002   jC813'.54   C2002-901501-4
PZ7

U.S. Publisher Cataloging-in-Publication Data
(Library of Congress Standards)

Jennings, Sharon.
Priscilla's paw de deux / by Sharon Jennings ; illustrated by Linda Hendry.—1st ed.
[36] p. : col. ill. ;   cm.
Summary: A rat's ambition to become a ballerina is tested when she discovers that a prowling watch cat also lives in the dance studio where she practices. But when Priscilla gets up the courage to confront her enemy, she finds they have something special in common.
ISBN 1-55041-718-5
ISBN 1-55041-720-7 (pbk.)
1. Courage -- Fiction. 2. Rats – Fiction. 3. Cats -- Fiction. I. Hendry, Linda. II. Title.
[E] 21   2002   AC CIP

Fitzhenry & Whiteside acknowledges with thanks the Canada Council for the Arts, the Government of Canada through the Book Publishing Industry Development Program (BPIDP), and the Ontario Arts Council for their support for our publishing program.

Printed in Hong Kong

Priscilla's Paw de Deux

By Sharon Jennings

Illustrated by Linda Hendry

Fitzhenry & Whiteside

Most days after work, Priscilla played her favorite music and danced all around her tiny home.

Afterward, she moaned about her bruised knees and groaned about her stubbed toes.

One night, Priscilla finally declared, "I need space! I must have room to dance!"

Over dinner, Priscilla complained to her friends.
As usual, they were gathered at Tony's Trattoria.
As always, they were seated at the best table
in the restaurant.

"And so, I'll have to move," concluded Priscilla.

"It'll be hard to find a bigger hole in the city," Cuthbert told her.

"Oh, Priscilla!" wailed Rosy. "You can't move away and leave me!"

"Oh, pooh!" said Priscilla. "I'll find something. You can help me look."

Priscilla and Rosy skipped work the next day and went hole-hunting. The first two apartments were far too small. The third looked promising, but then Rosy noticed a mother cat and five kittens. The two friends shuddered and scuttled off.

They fared no better the rest of the day. Discouraged, they stopped by Sugarman's Candy Store for a bite of something sweet.

It was then that they heard the music.

"Shhh!" Priscilla commanded. "Listen!"

Priscilla closed her eyes and swayed back and forth.

"Tchaikovsky," she explained.

"*Swan Lake* Ballet," she added. "Come on, Rosy!

I want to know who is playing that music."

Priscilla didn't have to look far. For there, above Sugarman's, was a sign that read, Madame Genevieve's Dance Studio.

Priscilla grabbed Rosy and ran up the stairs and down the hall and under the door of Madame Genevieve's.

Priscilla gasped in delight. All about her were huge mirrors and slippered feet.

For the next little while, Priscilla and Rosy watched boys and girls *jeté* and *plié*, *pointe tendu* and *pas de chat*.

Priscilla didn't once take her eyes off Madame Genevieve and her assistant Miss Tania.

All too soon, the class was over and Priscilla was back outside in the alley.

Trembling with excitement, she turned to her friend.

"I don't have to move after all. I am going to take dance lessons at Madame Genevieve's."

Priscilla hurried home to change.

It was very late, and Madame Genevieve's was deserted.
Priscilla laced up her pointe shoes and turned on the
music. She stood in front of the mirror and did everything
the children had done earlier.

And then, out of the corner of her eye and in the
middle of her pirouette, Priscilla saw a dark shape
spring from the shadows.

"EEEK!" squeaked Priscilla.

"MEOW!" meowed the cat.

Priscilla leaped for dear life around the studio.

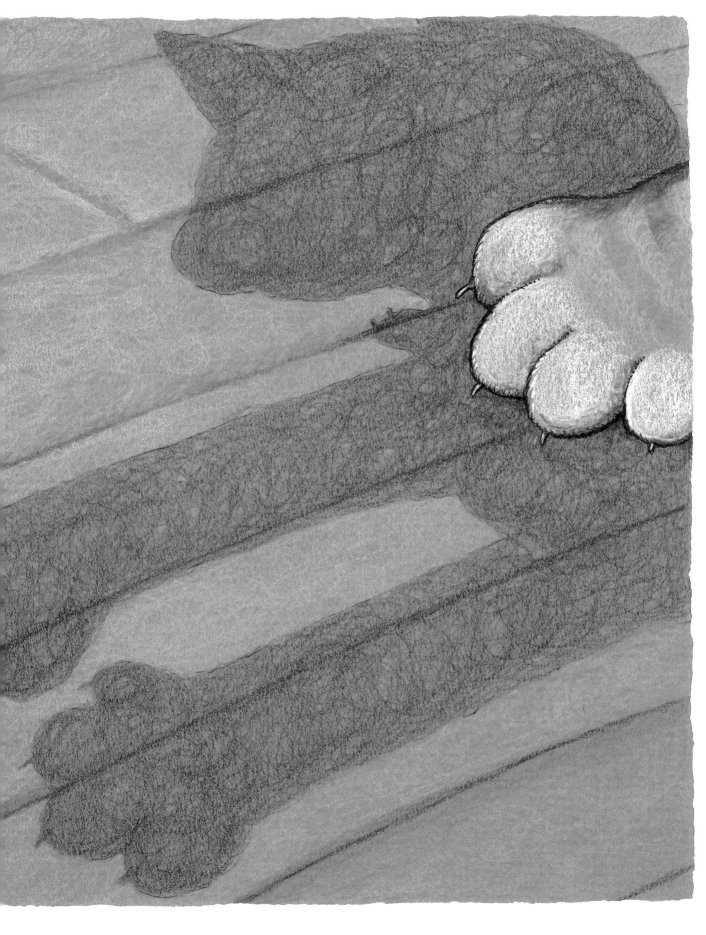

Heart thumping, Priscilla slid under Madame Genevieve's door and raced home. She shoved her bricks into place and collapsed on the sofa.

But as soon as Priscilla had calmed down, she got angry.

She stood up and shook her fist.

"No flea-bitten, mangy fur-ball of a watchcat is going to stop me from dancing!" she cried.

The next day, over crullers and café au lait, Priscilla told her friends her plan.

"Madame Genevieve's has a night watchcat," she explained. "But if you all come with me, then you can keep the cat busy chasing you in all directions while I practice."

Everyone stared at her.

"We really like you, Priscilla," Rudolph finally said. "But none of us wants to die just so you can dance."

Priscilla scowled and stomped off.

"Some friends you are!" she shouted back at them.

That afternoon, Priscilla left work early and headed to Madame Genevieve's. Once again she sat in the corner and watched the lessons. As soon as the last child had gone, Priscilla took her place at the barre. Her plan was to dance before the watchcat showed up.

Her plan worked.

At last, perspiring and tired, Priscilla took off
her shoes and packed her bag.

    She headed for the door...as the door slid open.

    Priscilla looked around desperately for a crack,
but saw no chance of escape.

    Terrified, she froze.

It was the watchcat. He stalked across the floor, turned on the music…and began to dance.

Priscilla stared, and then she scowled. She took a deep breath and marched over to the cat. He leaped—up on the barre.

"Don't come any closer!" he whimpered.

Priscilla stood in front of the cat.

"What's going on here?" she demanded.

"I'm Per…Per…Percival," he stammered,
"and I'm just here to dance. Please leave me alone."

Priscilla grinned.

"I'm Priscilla," she said. "We have to talk."
And then Priscilla held out her hand.

"I like the way you *jeté*," she told Percival.
"Maybe we could dance together."

Soon Priscilla and Percival were meeting at Madame Genevieve's four times a week.

It was Priscilla's idea that she and Percival
would put on a recital for their friends at the end
of the season.

The big night arrived, and rats and cats filled the auditorium. They all squeaked and purred together as Priscilla and Percival performed the Pas de Deux from *Swan Lake*.

"Oh, Priscilla! You are a beautiful dancer!"
exclaimed Rosy.

"Yes, I am," agreed Priscilla.

And she curtsied to her audience
again and again.

Priscilla's Dance Studio

Plié
bend at the knees

Pointe Tendu
stretch and point
the foot

Jeté
leap from one foot
to the other

Pas De Chat
step or jump like a cat

Pas De Deux
a dance for two